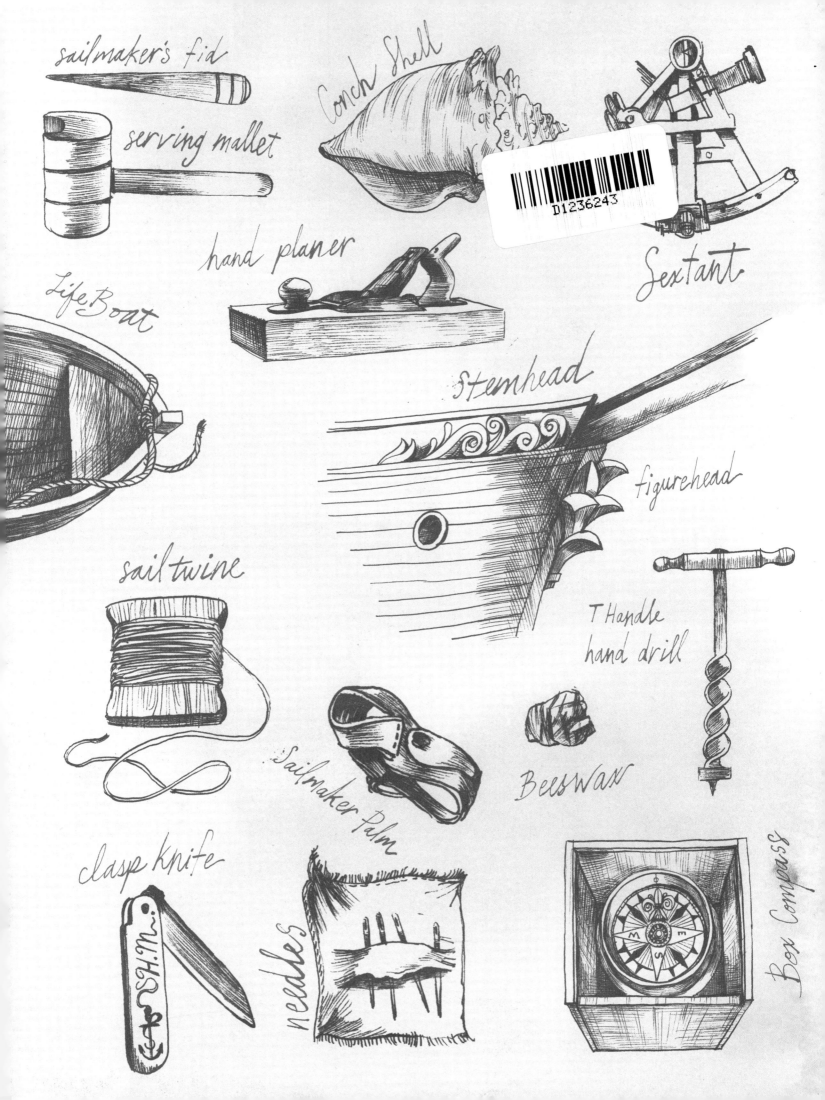

sailmaker's fid

serving mallet

Conch Shell

Sextant

hand planer

LifeBoat

Stemhead

figurehead

sail twine

T Handle
hand drill

Sailmaker Palm

Beeswax

clasp knife

needles

Box Compass

HOPE AT SEA

AN ADVENTURE STORY

DANIEL MIYARES

a·s·b

anne schwartz books

Whenever my world feels small,
I turn to the sea.

The new clipper ship is almost done.
That means Papa will be leaving soon.
He is the ship's carpenter and will keep it seaworthy on
the long voyage. Oh, how I wish I could join him!

I don't want to hear Papa's stories after he returns.

I want to be *part* of those stories.

I will stow away!

Now's my chance.

ALL ABOARD!

WEIGH ANCHOR!

MAKE SAIL!

There's no turning back now. I can hear the sails snap to attention and salute the wind as we pick up speed.

My stomach is in knots.
Will I be discovered?
Will Papa be angry with me?

The deck is a flurry of activity!
Everyone has a job to do, and every job
needs doing.

A sailor's life is harder than I thought, but I may be starting to get the hang of it.

Papa has shown me that even the smallest
twinkle of light can guide us.

Our course has been set. We travel for weeks.
The farther we go, the more cargo we load on board.

Sugar from the West Indies, and now coffee beans and cotton from Port Rio Grande.

The ship feels more and more like home.

I know the grain of each board like the freckles on my arm, and every piece of rigging like the braid of my hair.

I can tell the weather just by the tilt of the cabin or the creak of the hull.

My journal is full of new stories to share, but I miss Mama.

We're not far from port now. I can almost smell
the bread baking in her oven.

A storm is bearing down on us!

"Stay down below, Hope!"
Papa cries.
     But how can I, when even hands
as small as mine are needed?

ROCKS!
OFF THE
STARBOARD SIDE!

ABANDON SHIP!

Our boats are no match for this rough and angry sea.
Before us is only darkness.

Then a small light appears on the horizon.
Then another . . . and another . . . until there is a
wall of light guiding us home!

On the rocky cliffs stand wives and children.

And there is Mama!

I thought my daily duties at sea were tough, but Mama
runs a tight ship.

Every morning Papa goes down to the shore to collect wood from the wreckage. He has told me that our ship's story is not over yet. What could he mean?

Its wood is being used to build our new home by the ocean!
Papa might be done sailing the seven seas, but he still has an
important job to do, and so do I.

To keep the light shining.

Dedicated to Stella, for when the storms come.

All rights reserved. Published in the United States by Anne Schwartz Books,
an imprint of Random House Children's Books, a division of Penguin Random House LLC, New York.

Anne Schwartz Books and the colophon are trademarks of Penguin Random House LLC.

Visit us on the Web! rhcbooks.com

Educators and librarians, for a variety of teaching tools, visit us at RHTeachersLibrarians.com

Library of Congress Cataloging-in-Publication Data
Names: Miyares, Daniel, author, illustrator.
Title: Hope at sea / Daniel Miyares.
Description: First edition. | New York : Anne Schwartz Books, [2021] | Audience: Ages 4–8. | Audience: Grades K–1. |
Summary: A girl pursues her own adventures by stowing away on her father's clipper ship.
Identifiers: LCCN 2020046357 | ISBN 978-1-9848-9283-6 (hardcover) | ISBN 978-1-9848-9284-3 (library binding) |
ISBN 978-1-9848-9285-0 (ebook)
Subjects: CYAC: Stowaways—Fiction. | Seafaring life—Fiction. | Shipwrecks—Fiction.
Classification: LCC PZ7.M699577 Ho 2021 | DDC [E]—dc23

The text of this book is set in 17-point Centaur MT Pro.
The illustrations were rendered in pen and ink with watercolor.
Book design by Nicole de las Heras
MANUFACTURED IN CHINA
10 9 8 7 6 5 4 3 2 1
First Edition

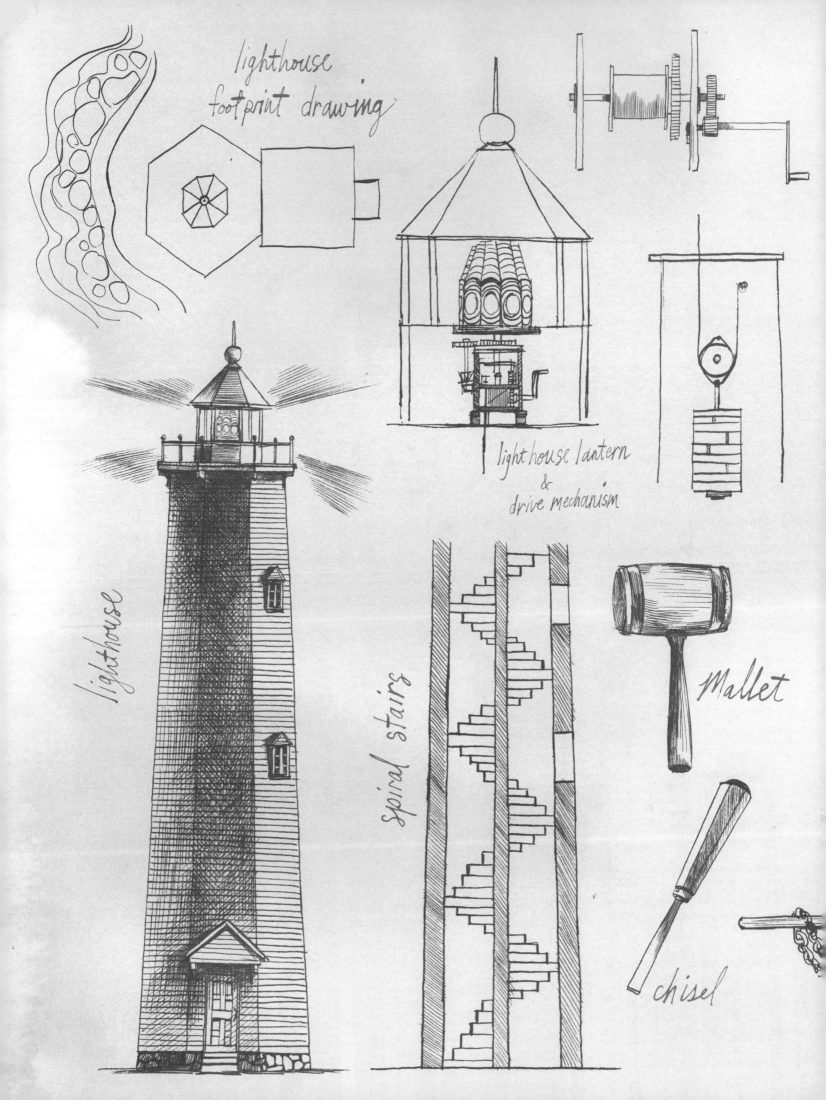

lighthouse
footprint drawing

lighthouse lantern
&
drive mechanism

lighthouse

spiral stairs

Mallet

chisel